for all the beautiful children

LETTER SOUND
YOGA

TATE PUBLISHING *& Enterprises*

DANETTE STEPHAN

Letter Sound Yoga
Copyright © 2011 by Danette Stephan. All rights reserved.

This novel is a work of fiction. Names, descriptions, entities, and incidents included in the story are products of the author's imagination. Any resemblance to actual persons, events, and entities is entirely coincidental.

The opinions expressed by the author are not necessarily those of Tate Publishing, LLC.

Published by Tate Publishing & Enterprises, LLC
127 E. Trade Center Terrace | Mustang, Oklahoma 73064 USA
1.888.361.9473 | www.tatepublishing.com

Tate Publishing is committed to excellence in the publishing industry. The company reflects the philosophy established by the founders, based on Psalm 68:11,
"The Lord gave the word and great was the company of those who published it."

Published in the United States of America

ISBN: 978-1-61777-807-0
1. Juvenile Fiction, Health & Daily Living, General
11.05.25

The purpose of this yoga practice is to help children master letters and their sounds while participating in a fun, creative, non-competitive physical fitness activity.

Our journey begins with two sun salutation A's followed by child's pose. Sun salutations are often done at the beginning of a yoga practice in order to warm up the muscles and increase the heart rate. During this practice children will flow through the esteem enhancing, brave warriors 1, 2 and 3, a few focusing and stilling poses, followed by some energy boosting heart openers. Finally there is a cool down sequence, which prepares the children for joyful focused learning. The entire sequence only takes about 30 minutes so it is perfect to do at the beginning of a class or at home.

In order for the children to succeed in mastering the letter sounds, they must repeat the name of the pose while doing it. All poses must be repeated on first the right side then the left.

The names of the poses are organized in such a way that the common letter sound comes first followed by the alternate sound followed by the beginning digraph. The vowels are organized with the short vowel sound first followed by the long.

Important tips for a successful yoga practice include being quiet, breathing through the nose and bringing your awareness to your own mind and body. There is no need to compare your poses to anyone else. As we are all different, so should the poses be. It is also important not to eat just before the yoga practice.

Now let's get ready to have some fun, learn and move!

SUN SALUTATION A

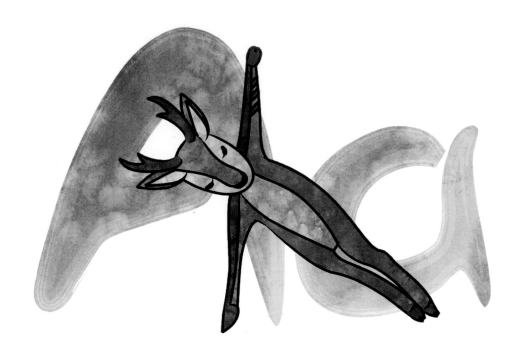

A Arrow with Angles

B   Bending Bow

C   Cat

Cow

Circle

Child

D Downward Dog

E   Endangered Eagle

F Frog

Folding

G Gorilla Growing Giant

H High Half Moon

Inverted Icicle

J

Jaguar Jumping

K King Dancer Knee Back

L Lightning Bolt Lifting

M Majestic Mountain

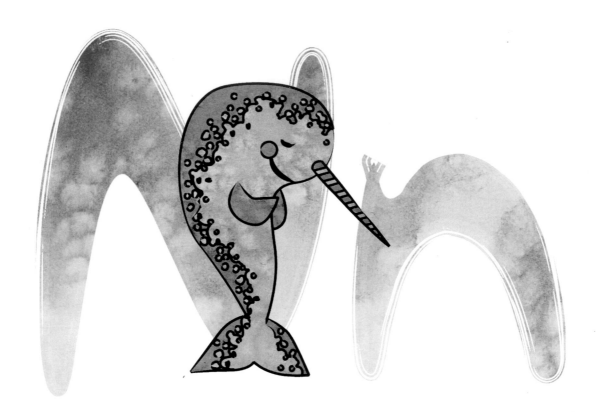

N

Namaste Nod

O

Offering Om
in Warrior One

P Pigeon in Peaceful Phase

Q

Quict Quail

R   Rock and Roll up to Ragdoll

S Standing Split and Shoulder Stand

T Two Warrior to ...

Triangle

Three Warrior to …

Tree

U Upward Pointing Unicorn

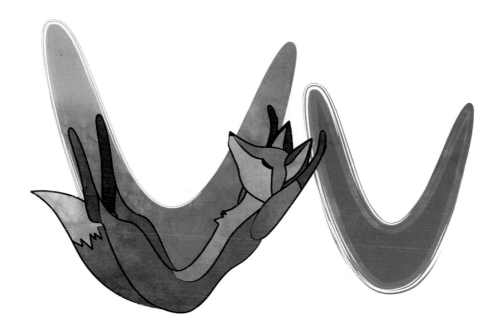

V

Vertical V

W   Wake up Wheel

X

Xiphoid Process
Rises and Falls in X

Y   Yogis Yawn in Y

Z

Zero Movement and Sound in Z

FINAL SEATED NAMASTE

ABOUT THE AUTHOR

Danette became a certified yoga teacher through Yoga Alliance after taking Jennifer Prugh's Joy of Yoga 200 hour teacher training. She has been teaching yoga to youth at Fuze in Los Gatos since 2008. Over the last few years she has taught a Vinyasa Flow yoga at Club One in Palo Alto, California, and at Master Edmonds Martial Arts Academy in Los Gatos, California. She currently teaches Vinyasa classes for both adults and teens at Breathe Los Gatos.

Equally thirsty to deepen her practice and knowledge of all branches of yoga, Danette continually attends conferences and takes workshops on topics as diverse as the history of yoga to breathing techniques and how yoga can benefit those who are physically challenged. As Danette believes that yoga is one of the greatest gifts she has ever received, she is passionate about returning it to all she is lucky enough to teach.

A native and current resident of Los Gatos, California, Danette's intense desire to teach children began almost two decades ago. Her dedication to deepen her education, and challenge herself compelled her to pursue a master's degree in education from San Jose State University. She has spent over eleven years teaching elementary school in the Campbell Union School District. She also shares her yoga practice with both staff and students at her school as well as contributing to the Art of Yoga Project (www.theartofyogaproject.org). Her passion for learning about new places and cultures has taken her to many places around the world. She lives in Los Gatos, California, with her husband and son and can be reached at http://www.danetteyoga.com.

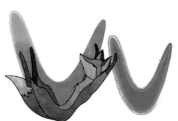

THE
END